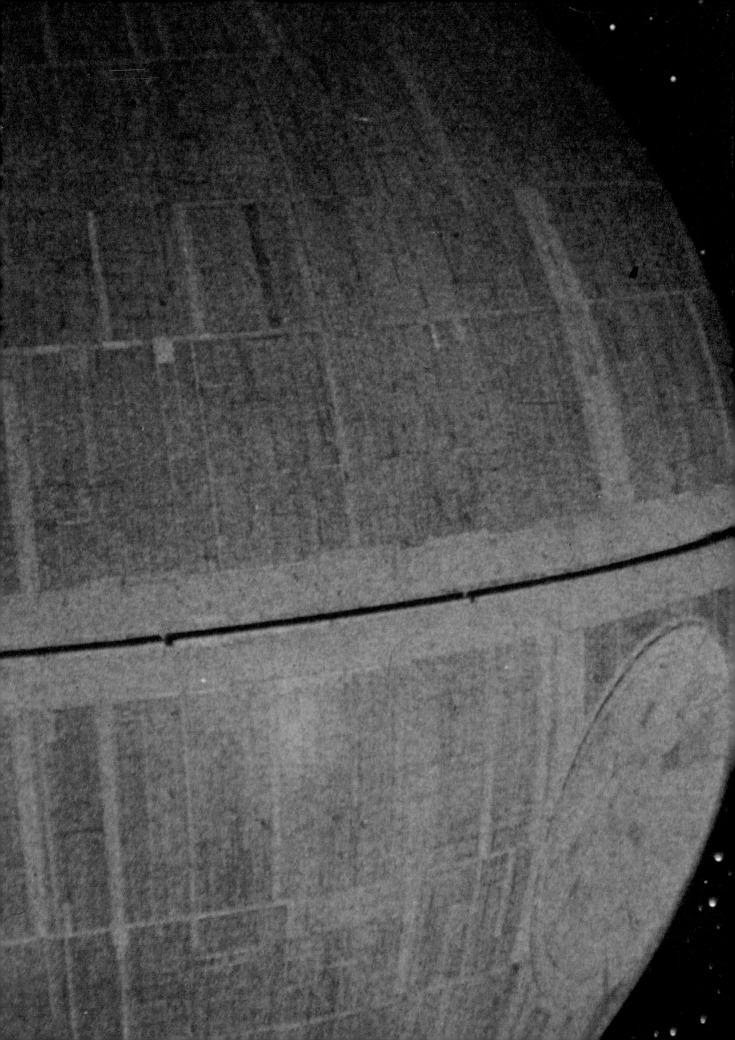

Based on the film by **George Lucas**

Story adapted by **Geraldine Richelson**

Designed and Edited by **Eleanor Ehrhardt**

Production Director **Edward McGill**

Director of Publications, Star Wars
Carol Wikarska

Special thanks to
Tom Cavallaro
Jerry Harrison
Sherry Holstein

Copyright © 1978 by The Star Wars Corporation. All rights reserved under International and Pan-American Copyright Conventions. Published in the United States by Random House, Inc., New York, and simultaneously in Canada by Random House of Canada Limited, Toronto.

Library of Congress Cataloging in Publication Data

Main entry under title:
The Star wars storybook.
    SUMMARY: The intergalactic adventures of Luke Skywalker and the Rebel Alliance as they battle the evil Imperial forces which have overthrown the Old Republic.   [1. Science fiction]   I. Star wars. [Motion picture]
PZ7.S7942   [Fic]   77-90196
ISBN 0-394-83785-1   ISBN 0-394-93785-6 lib. bdg.

Manufactured in the United States of America.   4 5 6 7 8 9 0

Photographs furnished by Twentieth Century-Fox

Han Solo Captain of the *Millennium Falcon*, a Corellian starship.

uke Skywalker A young farmer who lives with his aunt and uncle on the planet atooine.

See Threepio (C-3PO) A tall, humanlike robot who translates all kinds of languages, including the electronic speech of many robots.

Ben (Obi-wan) Kenobi A good and just warrior of the Old Republic who possesses a special power called the Force.

Chewbacca A two-hundred-year-old "Wookiee" whose language is only grunts and growls. He is co-pilot of the *Millennium Falcon*.

Darth Vader The evil Imperial Dark Lord who uses his special powers to try to crush the Rebellion.

rtoo - Detoo (R2-D2) A clever, computer ype of robot who speaks only in electronic ounds.

rincess Leia Organa A young Senator who is secretly leading the Rebellion against he evil Imperial forces.

Grand Moff Tarkin An Imperial Governor.

Death Star A gigantic and powerful satellite battle station built by fiendish Governor Tarkin to stop the Rebellion.

In another galaxy, in another time . . . on a planet named Tatooine lived a young man, Luke Skywalker. Luke longed for excitement. But Tatooine, millions of miles from the center of the galaxy, seemed far from the world of adventure.

Luke lived with his Uncle Owen and Aunt Beru. He eagerly awaited the time he could leave for the Academy on another planet. There he would join his friends and train to be a space pilot. Luke stayed home because his Uncle Owen needed his help on the farm, but his eyes were on the stars and his heart was far away.

Farming was difficult on Tatooine. Two blazing suns, called G1 and G2, kept the planet as hot and dry as a desert. The people on Tatooine could get water only by taking it from the atmosphere. And they needed machines called vaporators to coax the moisture from the air.

The vaporators had to be guarded from the roving, subhuman creatures on Tatooine—the jawas and the Tusken Raiders. The jawas spoke in strange hisses and grunts, and their eyes glowed. They traveled in large vehicles called sandcrawlers, collecting robots and scraps of machinery to sell. The Tusken Raiders were bigger and fiercer than the jawas. Raiders usually kept to themselves. But if they came into contact with humans, they were very dangerous.

One day, Luke was adjusting his uncle's vaporator with the help of a worn-out, broken-down robot named Treadwell. He glanced skyward to search for a cloud. Not a sign of one—nor would there be until he got the vaporator working again. But way up high a brilliant gleam of light caught his eye!

Luke grabbed his macrobinoculars for a better look. He wished he had a powerful telescope, but never mind! The binocs treated him to quite a show. Two silvery specks—skyships for sure—were exchanging heavy bursts of fire. The sky was exploding with red, blue, and green flashes of light.

If Luke had had the powerful telescope he longed for, he would have seen a small galactic cruiser racing through space on a wild, zigzag course. Zooming to the left! Zooming to the right! It looked as if the pilot had lost control—but no! He was skillfully dodging the red, blue, and green flashes of light that came from the weapons on a huge Imperial starship. The starship kept up the attack on the cruiser, and suddenly—though Luke was too far away to hear—there came the roar of an explosion, then another and another. The galactic cruiser shook as the flashing light beams finally hit their mark—the main solar fin. The battle was over. The Imperials pulled up alongside the cruiser.

Inside the corridor of the cruiser, two robots, Artoo Detoo and See Threepio, had been tossed around. See Threepio was tall and shaped like a human. His exterior, usually shiny and golden, was now covered with dust and dirt. And it was dented from having been thrown against walls and floors. Artoo Detoo was short and squat, with thick, sturdy legs that kept him better balanced than See Threepio. During the explosions, he had taken much less of a beating.

The two robots looked different from each other because they had been built for different purposes. Artoo, in his own way, was as skilled as Threepio. But because Threepio was more like a human, he fancied himself smarter than his smaller friend.

The tall robot was a worrier. Sometimes he nagged at Artoo, even scolded him, but he really didn't mean anything by it. Artoo was level-headed and dependable. The two were very good friends.

Though caught in the battle, the two robots did not know what the fighting was about any more than Luke did far below on Tatooine. They had never heard the history of the galaxy—of how the evil Imperial forces had overthrown the Old Republic, with its good laws and wise Senate. And they had never heard of the kind, protective Jedi knights, who had watched over the Republic for centuries until they were destroyed. Now, the power-mad Emperor of the Imperial forces ruled unjustly without regard for right and wrong. After many years of Imperial tyranny, a Rebel Alliance had formed. It was now fighting bravely to bring back the ideals of the Old Republic. The galactic cruiser on which Artoo and Threepio were traveling was one of the Rebel ships.

"Artoo, listen," Threepio said in his worried way. "The captain has shut down the main reactor and the drive. We'll be destroyed for sure. This is madness. Madness!"

Artoo stayed calm. His senses were slightly sharper than See Threepio's, and he used them now to figure out what was happening. As Artoo listened, he reported to See Threepio in his own mechanical language. Lights blinked and winked busily in his head as he beeped and chirped.

All at once, the crew of the Rebel ship dashed through the corridor. They looked worried, and they carried their rifles ready for action. As the crew disappeared around a corner, Artoo and Threepio heard firing. With a blinding flash, a big hole tore open in the roof of the corridor and the Imperials jumped through, firing as they came.

The robots ducked a barrage of deadly energy beams that shot past their heads. Smoke filled the corridor. In the confusion, Threepio and Artoo were separated.

The Imperials had boarded the ship. But the brave Rebels were not about to surrender without a fight. What a battle!

The Imperial officer leading the attack against the Rebel crew was a man feared by everyone, even his own troops. He was Darth Vader, Dark Lord of the Sith. Vader was taller than most men. He wore flowing black robes and his face was masked by a frightening black metal breath screen. Vader seemed surrounded by a cloud of evil. He strode through the corridor of the ship, passing—and ignoring—the robots.

When the smoke cleared, Threepio spotted Artoo at the far end of the corridor. A beautiful, white-robed human was leaning over Artoo, touching him with a small, graceful hand. Or was Threepio imagining her? The haze from the battle made it impossible to be sure.

When Threepio reached the end of the corridor, no human was in sight. He decided not to mention the white-robed human. He didn't want Artoo to think his wires were crossed and that he was not thinking logically.

"Well, Artoo," Threepio asked, "what are we going to do now? The Imperials will think we know something. They'll take us apart and use us for spare parts for other robots."

But Artoo wasn't listening. Ignoring Threepio's complaints, he headed down the passageway. Artoo marched halfway across the ship. Finally, he stopped in front of a lifepod hatch. Threepio caught up to him.

"We're not allowed in an emergency lifepod," said Threepio, greatly alarmed. "It's for humans only. Get away from there!"

As Artoo climbed into the pod, he chattered at Threepio in a rapid-fire series of beeps, whistles, gurgles, and whirs.

"Mission...what mission?" shouted Threepio. "You've gone mad! And don't call *me* a mindless twerp, you overweight blob of grease. I'm staying here."

Suddenly there was a deafening explosion. Threepio changed his mind in a hurry. He jumped into the lifepod. Artoo flipped switches, pushed buttons, and the two robots zoomed off into space.

Back in the Imperial ship, Darth Vader was seething. He was sure the Rebels had discovered the secret plans for Death Star, the powerful new Imperial space station. As soon as Death Star was completed, the Emperor and his evil forces would be able to use it as a base to rule the entire galaxy.

"Your ship comes from Alderaan," the Dark Lord thundered at a poor Rebel prisoner. "I know all about the World Family of Alderaan and the Alliance to Restore the Republic. Is any of the royal family on board? I know spies have transmitted information to your ship. I want to know what happened to those data tapes!"

The Rebel denied everything, saying only that his ship had been on a diplomatic mission. Vader whirled, faced his Imperial officers, and ordered, "Search that ship from end to end. Tear it apart if you must. But find those tapes! I must have those plans. And bring me all passengers—ALIVE!"

Imperial stormtroopers spread out to search the Rebel ship. As one of the troopers entered a small passageway, he saw a flutter of something white. What luck! Though he didn't know it, the trooper had discovered the Princess Leia Organa, member of the royal family, youngest member of the Imperial Senate, and the guiding force of the Rebellion. "Take her alive," the trooper commanded over his tiny condenser microphone. "Set your pistols on STUN."

The Princess shot first. ZRRAP! ZRRAP! Two troopers went down. Before she could shoot again, a bright-green ray from another trooper's gun hit her side, and she slumped to the deck.

Princess Leia woke to discover her hands tied behind her. The troopers marched her to a hallway, and up to the large hole that had been blown in the side of the ship. A passageway now led from this hole to the Imperial cruiser.

Suddenly, Darth Vader's dark shadow loomed large above the Princess. The Dark Lord was delighted. He had captured a very valuable prize. Princess Leia was startled, but she managed to look and sound calm. "So it's you, Darth Vader," she said. "The Imperial Senate will condemn you for attacking a diplomatic mission."

"Don't play games with me, Your Highness. This is no diplomatic mission. You are a traitor. You have been in contact with Rebel spies and they have transmitted a set of secret plans to you. Where are the tapes that carry that information?"

"I don't know what you're talking about," said the Princess. "I'm a member of the Senate. I have no secret tapes."

"You're lying," Vader snapped. "You're part of the Rebel Alliance." Turning to his officers, he said grimly, "Take her away."

An Imperial trooper reported to Vader, "We searched the Rebel ship, sir. We found no tapes, and nothing has left the ship but a lifepod with no life forms aboard."

The report did not satisfy Vader. He answered, "There might not have been life forms in that pod, but it could have carried the tapes we're looking for. Send a party to find that pod."

Inside the pod, as Artoo prepared to land on the hot yellow surface of Tatooine, Threepio feared for his mechanical life. "Are you sure you know how to pilot this thing?" he called out. His question was answered by a series of bumps and thumps and quivers. The pod had landed! The robots' circuits might never be the same, but both were in one piece. They were in a barren place, with sandstone ridges in one direction and mile after mile of sand dunes in all others.

Threepio headed toward the dunes, moaning as he marched. "We must have been made to suffer. I'm still shaking from that headlong crash you called a landing! I've got to rest." But Artoo Detoo refused to rest, and he turned sharply and started off toward the ridges.

"Hey," Threepio yelled. "Where do you think *you're* going?" Artoo answered with a stream of blips and bleeps, whirs and whistles. Threepio didn't like what he heard. "It's too rocky over there," he declared. "I'm going this way. And when you get into trouble, don't come to me begging for help."

For hours, Threepio trudged up and down the dunes. His thermostat was overheating. His joints were grinding from the sand. "This is all your fault," he shouted at Artoo, who was much too far away to hear. At that moment, way off in the distance, Threepio spotted some sort of vehicle. It was coming towards him! A ride! He was about to be rescued! . . . or so he thought.

The pod had landed on Tatooine not far from where Luke Skywalker was having an unexpected reunion with his friend Biggs. Biggs was on a visit from the Academy, and Luke wanted to hear all about it. The two friends talked and laughed for a while.

Then Biggs got serious. "Luke, I have to tell someone, and you're my best friend. As soon as I get back, I'm going to join the Rebel Alliance."

Luke was startled. Fun-loving, happy-go-lucky Biggs was going to be one of the Rebels! "You can't do it, Biggs. You'll never make contact with a Rebel unit. You'll be captured by the Imperials. You'll…"

"You don't know how bad things are, kid," Biggs interrupted. "Only the threat of Rebellion keeps the Imperials from being even more evil. Out here on Tatooine, you don't hear much about the terrible things the Empire does. The Rebellion is growing, and I want to fight for the side I believe in."

The friends said a sad good-bye, Luke returning to the farm and Biggs going off to fight for his beliefs. Luke couldn't remember ever feeling so alone.

Spurred on by his mission, Artoo continued his lonely journey, climbing recklessly over the rocky land. He was so determined to reach a human settlement and deliver his precious message that he didn't notice the tiny figures on the cliffs above him. ZAP! A light beam hit him and he tumbled. A ripple of fluorescent light, a short electronic squeak—and Artoo fell over, completely still, except for his front lights, which kept blinking wildly.

Three jawas scurried towards him. Their eyes glowed as they jabbered. They would have no trouble selling this robot. Other jawas joined them, and they dragged Artoo back to their enormous sandcrawler. They rolled him over to a large tube that extended from the sandcrawler, and with a great WHOOSH he was vacuumed into the vehicle.

Artoo landed in a small room loaded with piles of scrap metal, broken instruments, and various kinds of robots. Over all the squeaks and squawks of robots he heard an excited shout. "Artoo Detoo! It's you! It's you!" It was Threepio—he, too, had been captured. Threepio stumbled through the scrap and hugged his little friend.

On Death Star, the powerful new battle station, the Imperial leaders were holding a meeting. General Tagge, a young man who hated Darth Vader, said angrily, "The Rebels are more dangerous than any of you think. They have good ships and pilots. They also have the plans of the battle station, thanks to Lord Vader, who has not been able to find the data tapes. He has not found the location of the hidden Rebel fortress, either."

Vader was infuriated. Governor Tarkin spoke. "Even with the information," he said, "the Rebels can't invade this station. It is far too powerful. Anyway, Lord Vader will soon find the Rebel fortress, and we will crush the Rebellion."

While the sandcrawler bounced along, Artoo shut down all his systems and rested. Threepio spent the time worrying about what the jawas would do to him and his friend. He hoped he and Artoo would not be melted down and used as scrap metal.

At last the sandcrawler stopped. Threepio woke Artoo. The jawas appeared and pushed Artoo, Threepio, and three other robots out of the machine onto the sands of Tatooine. Threepio looked around and saw small domes and vaporators. *Humans must live here*, he thought. Perhaps we will be saved!

While Threepio was thinking, Luke and his Uncle Owen approached the sandcrawler. They needed two robots for the farm work. While the jawas jabbered, Uncle Owen chose a robot who looked a lot like Artoo. Then he stopped in front of Threepio. "Do you understand moisture vaporators?" he asked. "I certainly do," Threepio answered.

"O.K.," Uncle Owen said to the jawas. "I'll take this one and the one back there." He paid the jawas and turned to his nephew. "Luke, take the robots to the garage. Have them cleaned up by suppertime."

As Luke walked away, he heard a sad little beep. Artoo didn't want to be left with the jawas. Threepio wished he could do something to save his friend. In a minute, he got his chance. PING! PING! The other robot Uncle Owen had picked suddenly started to pop his parts.

"If I may say so, sir," Threepio whispered to Luke, "that Artoo unit is in top condition." He pointed to Artoo Detoo. "Don't let the sand and dust fool you. You ought to swap." Luke convinced Uncle Owen, Uncle Owen convinced the jawas, and in a few minutes the two friends were together again. In Uncle Owen's garage, Threepio took a much-needed lubrication bath, and Artoo plugged into a large power unit and recharged himself.

When the robots were refreshed, Luke unplugged Artoo and noticed a small metal fragment jammed between two wires. "I'd better remove that metal," he said. CRACK! WHACK! A sudden shock sent Luke reeling. A small image of a beautiful girl appeared in front of Artoo.

The image spoke. "Obi-wan Kenobi," the girl pleaded, "help me. You're my only hope." Luke stared, dumbfounded, as she said the same thing over and over.

"She's beautiful. Who is she?" he demanded of Artoo. "What's this all about?"

Artoo let out an innocent beep, pretending to be as surprised as Luke. Threepio tried to answer, but he didn't know what was happening. He thought the girl might be the person he had seen leaning over Artoo on the Rebel ship. He told Luke she might be someone important, but he wasn't sure. Poor Threepio! He tried to get Artoo to explain, but Artoo refused. In a series of beeps and whistles, the small robot said he belonged to Obi-wan Kenobi and would give the message only to him.

Threepio was worried. He told Luke what Artoo had said. "I'm afraid his logic circuits are confused, sir," he apologized.

"Obi-wan Kenobi," Luke mumbled. "I wonder if that could be old Ben Kenobi, the hermit who lives on the Western Dunes. We should do something to help that beautiful girl. She seems to be in some kind of trouble. There must be more to that message."

Luke reached for Artoo, but the robot backed up rapidly, squeaking and sputtering. "Sir," said Threepio, "he says if you remove his restraining bolt, he'll be able to repeat the entire message."

Luke decided Artoo was too small to run away, so he removed the bolt. ZZZIP! The girl disappeared as suddenly as she had come. "Where is she?" demanded Luke. "Bring her back." But Artoo whistled innocently. Fortunately for Artoo, Aunt Beru called Luke to dinner and the robots were left alone.

While Aunt Beru served dinner, Luke told Uncle Owen he thought the Artoo unit might have been stolen. "He keeps saying he belongs to Obi-wan Kenobi. Do you think he means old Ben?"

Uncle Owen answered Luke angrily. "You forget about Ben Kenobi, do you hear? That robot couldn't possibly belong to him."

However, Luke didn't want to forget. "But Uncle Owen," he went on. "Suppose this Obi-wan person comes looking for the robot?"

"I don't think he will, Luke," Uncle Owen said more gently. "I think Obi-wan died about the same time your father did."

Luke changed the subject. "Uncle Owen," he said, "if the two new robots work out well, I'd like to leave for the Academy."

Uncle Owen answered the way he always did. "Next year, Luke."

Luke ran out of the house, and Aunt Beru said quietly, "You can't keep him here much longer, Owen. He's like his father."

"That's what I'm afraid of," Uncle Owen answered.

When Luke got back to the garage, he found Threepio all upset—and all alone. Artoo had run away! "His wires must be crossed, sir," Threepio said sadly. "I've never known him to do anything like this before. Can we go after him?"

"It's too dangerous at night," Luke answered. "We'll go in the morning. I hope we find him. Uncle Owen will be furious."

Early the next morning, Luke and Threepio set out in Luke's landspeeder to look for Artoo. Luke knew there might be some trouble from the Tusken Raiders. But he didn't sense the greater danger in store for him.

Luke and Threepio were far into the deserted wasteland when then they finally spotted Artoo. Unfortunately, the Tusken Raiders had already spotted *them*. The Tuskens were following the landspeeder on their Banthas, great beasts that looked like dinosaurs.

Luke and Threepio took turns scolding Artoo. The poor little fellow beeped sadly about his mission, but Threepio wouldn't listen. Just as they were starting to get back in the landspeeder the Tuskens attacked. One of them hit Luke over the head. Threepio went tumbling down the side of a sand dune. Artoo Detoo squeezed between two big rocks. Then surprisingly, the Tuskens stood motionless. A low, booming sound rolled through the canyon. The ghostlike hollow cry terrified the Tuskens. They ran to their Banthas, climbed on, and disappeared.

Artoo was afraid of something worse than the Tusken Raiders. He had never heard such a howl. But when he felt brave enough to peek out, he saw a pleasant-looking old man. The man bent over Luke and called out to Artoo. "Hello, there, my little friend. No need to be afraid." Luke soon woke up, rubbing his head and wondering what had happened. "Rest a minute," the man said. "You're lucky you're in one piece."

Luke recognized him. "Ben!" he said excitedly. "Ben Kenobi! Am I glad to see you!" He rambled on, telling Ben about Artoo and his mission and the image of the beautiful girl. "He says he belongs to someone called Obi-wan Kenobi. Is that a relative of yours? My uncle says he's dead."

The man smiled. "No, he's not dead, Luke. And not a relative. I am Obi-wan Kenobi. I haven't used that name in a long time."

Just then, Artoo beeped and whirled around. "Threepio!" shouted Luke. "I almost forgot."

The poor robot was lying at the bottom of a sand dune. All his systems had stopped. One of his arms was broken off. Luke flipped a switch on Threepio's back and he started to hum again.

"Let's get out of here, Luke," Obi-wan said. "The Raiders may come back. We can repair Threepio at my cave, and I can find out more about Artoo's mission."

At the cave, Luke fixed Threepio up as good as new. Then he watched as Ben Kenobi fiddled with Artoo. ZZZING! The beautiful girl appeared again and spoke.

"General Obi-wan Kenobi, I present myself in the name of the World Family of Alderaan and the Alliance to Restore the Republic. Your friend, my father, begs you to help us as you did many years ago. The Imperials have captured me. I have put the secret plans into the mind of this robot. Please take him to my father on Alderaan. Please do not fail us."

Luke's mind was spinning. Old Ben . . . a general? a hero? He gasped. Ben spoke quietly. "I was a Jedi knight, Luke. So was your father. Your Uncle Owen didn't want you to know. He wanted you to stay on the farm."

"What was my father like?" Luke asked.

"He was a good friend, a smart fighter, and the best pilot I ever knew. The Force was strong in him. I think you're like your father, Luke."

As soon as he said that, Obi-wan took a small device from a drawer and handed it to Luke. "Your father's lightsaber. He wanted you to have it when you were old enough."

Luke knew lightsabers had been the special weapons of the Jedi knights. "How did my father die?" he asked.

Kenobi looked away. Very slowly he said, "A young Jedi named Darth Vader, a boy I was training, murdered him. Vader used his knowledge of the Force for evil."

"What is this Force you keep talking about?" Luke asked.

"It is hard to explain, Luke. The Force is an energy, a power that surrounds us. If you learn to put it to work for you, you can be as strong as a Jedi. I'll teach you more about it as we travel to Alderaan."

Luke jumped. "Alderaan! I can't go with you. I must get home. My uncle will be looking for me."

There was a long silence.

"Well," said Luke, "I guess I could take you as far as Anchorhead. You can get a ride to Mos Eisley from there. You'll find a spaceship at Mos Eisley to take you to Alderaan."

"That's a beginning," answered Ben. "You have to do what you think is right. Let's get started."

As Luke and Ben were racing along in the landspeeder, Ben suddenly pointed beyond the dunes. "Luke, over there—smoke!

Let's take a look. Someone may be in trouble." Luke turned the speeder around and they entered a canyon filled with destruction. The remains of a jawa sandcrawler and several dead jawas lay next to clearly visible Bantha tracks.

"The Tusken Raiders must have done this," said Luke.

"That's what someone wanted us to think," said Ben. "But only Imperial troops could have destroyed something this big. And look at those tracks, Luke. Tuskens ride their Banthas single file so that no one will know how many of them there are. These tracks are side by side."

Luke became alarmed. "These may be the same jawas who sold us the robots. The Imperials must have been looking for Artoo. They may have traced him to Uncle Owen!"

Luke jumped into his landspeeder and roared off at full speed. As he neared his home, billowing smoke darkened the sky. Luke stumbled though the smoke, not believing what he saw: his home—totally destroyed by fire! Aunt Beru and Uncle Owen—dead! Luke fell to the ground, buried his face in the sand, and cried.

Darth Vader was still trying to decide what to do about the Princess. Even though he had had her tortured, she had told him nothing.

"I think I know a better way to get information from Princess Leia," Governor Tarkin announced. "It's time to demonstrate the full power of this station." He turned to one of his officers. "Set course for the Alderaan system."

Moments later a Commander reported to Darth Vader. "Troopers are searching Tatooine now. We'll have those robots soon, sir."

"Send in as many men as you need," Vader ordered. "We must get those data tapes."

Luke drove slowly back to Kenobi and the robots. The minute Ben saw the boy's face, he knew what had happened. "I share your sorrow," he said quietly.

Words poured out of Luke's mouth, "I'll take you to Mos Eisley, Ben. There's no longer any reason for me to stay here. I want to go with you to Alderaan. I want to learn about the Force. I want to be a Jedi knight like my father."

And so, Ben and Luke and the two robots set a course for Mos Eisley. When they reached the big spaceport city, Ben cautioned Luke. "This is a rough place, full of dangerous characters. And I'm sure the Imperials will be looking for Artoo Detoo. We must be very careful."

As they entered the city, Imperial troops stopped them. "How long have you had these robots?" one of them demanded. "Three or four seasons," Luke answered nervously.

"They're for sale if you want them," Kenobi added.

The Imperial trooper ignored him. "Let me see your identification," he said to Luke.

When Kenobi spoke again, his voice sounded strange. Looking straight at the trooper, he said slowly, "You don't need to see his identification."

With the blank stare of a hypnotized man, the trooper said, "We don't need to see his identification."

Then Kenobi spoke again. "These are not the robots you're looking for."

"These are not the robots we're looking for," said the trooper. "Move along."

Luke couldn't believe it. "How did you do that?" he asked Ben.

"The Force, Luke. It's a powerful friend. Of course, it can also be dangerous if it is not used properly."

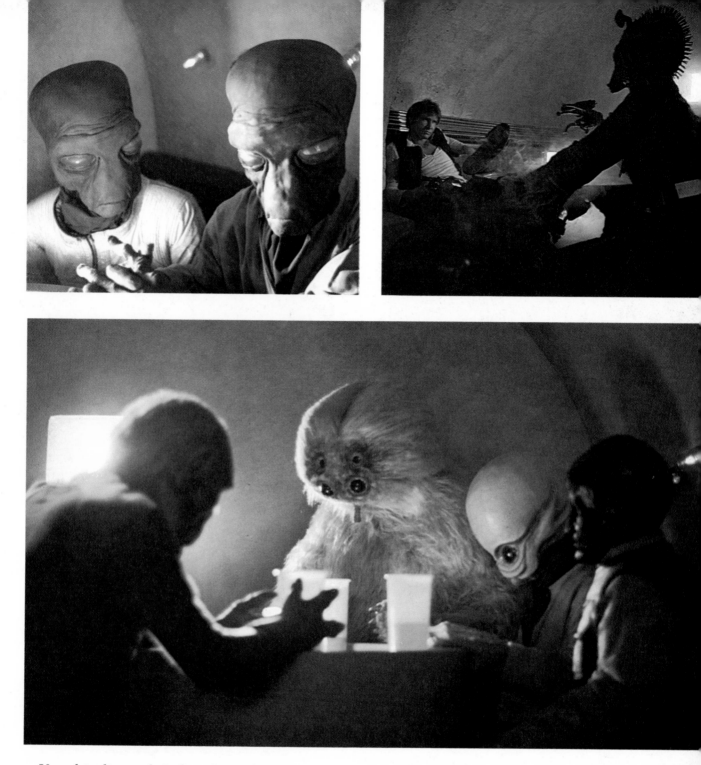

Kenobi directed Luke through the streets of Mos Eisley to a cantina where space pilots often spent their leisure time. The cantina was full of scary-looking characters—Luke had never seen so many. Ben pointed to one group. "They're Corellians, Luke. Very good, experienced pilots. Stay here. I'll be back in a minute."

Some tough-looking creatures came up to Luke, itching for a fight. They insisted Artoo and Threepio leave the cantina. Luke wanted to avoid trouble so he sent the robots outside. But three of the creatures were still eager to fight and pulled out pistols. Ben Kenobi suddenly appeared next to Luke. As he did, one of the creatures hit Luke, sending him sprawling across the floor. Then he pointed a blaster at Ben. There was a flash of blue light as Ben's lightsaber killed the creature. Everyone in the place, including Luke, was amazed at the old man's superhuman speed and strength.

Maria de Aragon 'Greedo'

When the cantina quieted down, a huge, hairy figure that looked like a giant ape headed toward Ben. "Luke, this is Chewbacca. He's a Wookiee. He's first mate on a space freighter that may be able to take us to Alderaan. He'll introduce us to the captain, a Corellian."

Chewbacca led them to a rear booth. He mumbled to a young man who greeted them. "Hello," he said pleasantly, "I'm Han Solo, captain of the spaceship *Millennium Falcon.* You're pretty handy with that saber. I hear you're looking for passage to Alderaan."

"Is your ship fast?" Kenobi asked.

"The fastest. What's your cargo?"

"Just myself and Luke and two robots. We want only two things—no questions and no trouble from the Imperials."

"It's a dangerous trip," said Solo. "But I owe money to one of these nasty characters, so I'll do it. It'll cost you ten thousand. And I want it in advance."

"What?" Luke gasped. "We could buy our own ship for that! I'm not such a bad pilot myself, you know."

Ben continued calmly. "We don't have that much," he said. "We can give you two thousand in advance. When we get to Alderaan, the government there will give you fifteen thousand more."

"O.K.," Solo said. "Be at docking bay ninety-four first thing in the morning." Then he added quickly, "And now, go. There are Imperial troopers in the doorway. They may be looking for you."

The Imperials *were* looking for Ben and Luke, who slipped out without being spotted.

Outside, Ben told Luke he didn't have the two thousand. "You'll have to sell your landspeeder, I'm afraid."

"That's O.K., Ben. I don't think I'll ever come back to this planet." Ben and Luke went to sell the speeder, and didn't notice the short, dark creature watching them.

The speeder sold, the money in hand, Luke, Ben, Artoo, and Threepio found their way to docking bay ninety-four. They still didn't see their small, dark pursuer,

who was now speaking rapidly into a small transmitter. Their eyes were on Chewbacca. He was waving excitedly. As the foursome hurried along, Luke looked around the shabby docking bay. It was old and run-down. The ship Chewbacca led them to looked even worse. "What a piece of junk," Luke muttered. "We'll never get to Alderaan on that thing."

Han Solo met them. As if he had heard Luke, he said, "The *Falcon* may not look like much, but she's all go. She can make point five beyond light speed."

Just then Chewbacca bounded up. Babbling to Solo, he charged into the ship. "We seem to be a bit rushed," Solo said. "Let's go!"

The others climbed aboard. Chewbacca squeezed into the pilot's seat and flipped some switches. The ship started to hum. The small, dark creature ran through the docking bay. Armed Imperial troops followed, firing on the *Millennium Falcon.*

"Quick, Chewie," yelled Solo, "deflector shields! Get us out of here." Solo pushed the quick-release button. The ship was off! One of the Imperials shouted into a communicator: "Flight deck, flight deck... they're escaping. Send out the destroyers."

Han Solo and Chewbacca watched the complicated instruments on the control panel. Suddenly Chewie saw something on the tracking screen. He growled and grunted and pointed his finger. Solo nodded. "I know, I know. Destroyers. Somebody certainly doesn't like our passengers. Hold those ships off, Chewie, while I get our ship ready for the jump into hyperspace."

"What did you two do?" Solo asked Luke and Ben. "We've got five destroyers on our tail."

"Can't you outrun them?" Luke asked him sarcastically. "I thought you said this ship was fast."

"Just watch it, kid," snapped Solo. "We'll be safe enough once we've made the jump into hyperspace. We'll be at supralight speed and they won't be able to track us."

Shots from a destroyer exploded around the *Falcon.*

"How long before you can make the jump?" Kenobi asked Solo.

"A few minutes. We can't rush it, or the ship might split."

Back in the main area of the ship, Threepio clung to his seat and muttered to Artoo Detoo, "Was this trip really necessary?"

The deadly space station, Death Star, entered the Alderaan system. Governor Tarkin sent for Princess Leia. "Well, Princess," Tarkin began. "You have been very stubborn. Despite all Lord Vader's attempts . . ."

The Princess interrupted him. "Torture, you mean."

Tarkin smiled. "Call it what you will. You have not told us the location of the Rebel base. Now you will witness the power of this battle station. We are about to demonstrate our strength by blowing up your home planet of Alderaan."

The Princess gasped. "No, no. You can't. Alderaan is a peaceful world."

"If you wish to save Alderaan, then tell us where the Rebel base is."

The Princess was beaten. To save Alderaan, she whispered, "Dantooine."

Governor Tarkin looked at Darth Vader in triumph. "There, you see, Lord Vader, the Princess can be very reasonable. Gentlemen," he announced to the other officers in the room, "when we finish our test explosion on Alderaan, we will proceed to Dantooine."

"What!" Princess Leia shouted. "But you said . . ."

Governor Tarkin laughed. "You shouldn't have believed me. We will destroy Alderaan as planned. Then we shall deal with Dantooine. Gentlemen, make sure the Princess has a perfect view."

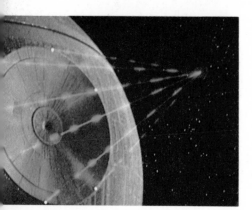

At the same time, aboard the *Millennium Falcon,* Obi-wan Kenobi shuddered and turned pale. "What is it, Ben?" Luke asked. "Are you all right?"

Kenobi answered softly, "I felt a sudden ebbing of the Force, as if a great source of energy had come to an end. I'm not sure what it was, exactly."

"Well," said Han Solo, "I have news that will make you feel better, old man. We've outrun the destroyers. We're on a straight course for Alderaan."

Over in one corner of the room, Three-pio was watching Chewbacca and Artoo play a kind of chess. They were moving strange, three-dimensional figures that hovered above light squares on a table. Chewie looked very pleased with himself as he waited for Artoo to make a move.

Artoo tapped his computer monitor, and one of the figures marched across the table to a new square.

Chewie stared at the table for a moment, then let out a loud, angry stream of sounds. Threepio scolded him. "Artoo made his move fair and square. Screaming about it won't help you."

Solo offered a word of advice. "Better let him win. It's not wise to upset a Wookiee."

Threepio began to explain to Chewbacca about good sportsmanship. Solo smiled. "I hope you'll both remember that when Chewie is pulling your arms off!"

"Yes, I see what you mean," said Three-pio. "Well, on second thought, sir, it would probably be *poor* sportsmanship for Artoo to take advantage of someone in a weak-ened position."

Kenobi and Luke paid no attention to the discussion. Luke was clipping the air with his activated lightsaber. Ben was giving him instructions. "No, Luke, not so choppy. Try to feel the Force. It will direct you."

"Is the Force an energy field?" Luke asked.

"Yes, and something more. It is a nothingness that can work miracles. Once you feel it the way the Jedi knights did, you won't need an explanation."

With that, Ben tossed a silvery globe about the size of a fist toward Luke. The globe stopped a few meters from the boy. Controlled by sensors, it could move swiftly. Luke lunged for it with the lightsaber. It darted behind him and sent out a thin light, which touched the back of Luke's thigh. Luke fell.

Solo laughed. "What hocus-pocus! Give me a good blaster any day."

"You don't believe in the Force?" Luke asked, as he got back to his feet.

"Not me. I control my own destiny. I wouldn't follow that old man so blindly, if I were you. He's full of tricks."

Kenobi smiled kindly and went on with Luke's lesson. "Try again, Luke. Relax. Let your mind drift. Stop thinking. Let the Force lead you."

Solo watched as Ben covered Luke's head with a helmet. "I can't see," Luke protested. "How can I fight?"

"With the Force," Ben explained. He talked soothingly. The globe bobbed in the air around Luke. Luke swung and missed. The globe got behind him and sent out one of its red beams. WHAM! It hit Luke right in the seat of his pants! Ben kept talking quietly. "Relax. Be free. Trust yourself." This time, Luke's lightsaber hit its mark.

"You see, Luke, you *can* do it." Ben was pleased. "I knew you were like your father."

"I'd call it luck," Solo sneered, and he went to check his instruments. "We're coming to Alderaan. Come on, Chewie. Let's prepare to land."

Suddenly, the *Millennium Falcon* began to shake. Asteroids were flashing everywhere. The sky was a blaze of lights. But something was missing—Alderaan.

"Missing? That's impossible!" Luke cried.

"Look for yourself," Solo said. "With all that wild energy outside, I'd say Alderaan's been blown up."

"But how? It would take thousands of ships," Luke protested.

A light flashed on the control panel, and an alarm sounded. "A ship close by," Solo announced.

It was a TIE fighter—an Imperial ship! But where had it come from? It couldn't have followed them in hyperspace—it was a short-range spaceship. It needed a base, and there was no Imperial base near Alderaan. Solo had to destroy that spaceship or the pilot would report the *Falcon* to the Imperials. As he chased the ship through space one star became brighter and brighter. "He's headed for that moon," Solo shouted.

"That's no moon," Kenobi said. "That's a space station. Turn this ship around. Let's get out of here."

Solo tried but it was too late. A powerful tractor beam caught the *Millennium Falcon*, pulling it closer and closer to the space station. Within minutes, the freighter vanished into an entryway of a gigantic battle station. It had landed on Death Star!

In another part of the space station, an officer reported to Tarkin and Vader. "Our scouts have checked Dantooine. They found no Rebel base."

"The Princess lied to us," Tarkin shouted. Before Tarkin and Vader could decide on their next move, an announcement came over the loudspeaker. "We've captured the freighter that left Mos Eisley."

"What does this mean, Vader?" Tarkin asked.

"It means we are about to recover the stolen data tapes. Our troubles are over."

At the docking bay the Imperials conducted a careful search of the captured *Millennium Falcon*. The Commander reported to Darth Vader. "The freighter was deserted." Vader, however, was convinced something was wrong. He had two guards remain with the *Falcon* and sent for a team of technicians to recheck the freighter.

Aboard the *Falcon*, Solo and his passengers had hidden themselves in a secret compartment under the floor. They heard Vader's orders over the intercom and clambered out of their hiding places. "Whew...lucky you built those secret compartments," Luke said. "But now what?"

Solo answered. "We'll clobber the guards, take their uniforms and get out of here. Here come the technicians now." WHAM! CRASH! Solo worked fast and efficiently. The noise alerted the guards, who raced up the ramp and into the freighter. Solo and Luke made short work of them, too. They quickly put on the guards' uniforms. Han and Luke escorted Chewie, Ben, and the robots off the freighter. "Hurry up," directed Solo, "this way ..."

They ran down a corridor and into a computer room. Kenobi walked over to a large computer panel and skillfully operated it. In minutes he had a map of Death Star on the screen. "Plug in Artoo," Ben said. "He'll be able to locate the power unit that operates the tractor beam. When he finds it, I'll disconnect it. There it is ... that's the information I need. Luke and Han, you stay here and guard the robots. We *must* deliver them to the Rebels or many more worlds will be blown up. Trust in the Force and wait." With one last look at the screen, Kenobi left.

No sooner was he gone than the computer began winking and blinking, whistling and hooting. So did Artoo Detoo. Threepio explained, "It's the Princess. He's found her. She's on station level five. Prisoner block AA-twenty-three. They're going to kill her!"

"Han, we've got to rescue her," Luke cried.

Solo shook his head. "Not me. I'm not going into an Imperial prison block."

Luke tried every argument he could think of, but Han refused. Then he remembered—Han needed money. "The Rebels will pay a reward," he said. That did it.

Luke and Han planned their attack. "See Threepio," said Luke, "you and Artoo wait here. We'll handcuff Chewie and pretend we're taking him to a cell."

"Pardon me, sir," Threepio said in a worried tone. "What should Artoo and I do if someone finds us here?"

"Hope he doesn't have a blaster," was Solo's reply.

When Luke and Han reached the prison area, they were stopped by a group of guards. "Where are you taking *that*?" one of them asked, pointing to Chewie.

"We're transferring a prisoner," Luke replied.

"I wasn't notified," the officer said. "I'll have to check."

"Uh-oh," said Solo, taking the handcuffs off Chewbacca. "Blast everything!" The officer tried to sound the alarm. Luke shot him, but the noise from the blasters had already alerted other troopers.

Solo shouted, "Hurry up, Luke. Find this Princess of yours. We're about to have company. Chewie and I will hold them off."

Luke raced from cell to cell. Finally, he found the right one—there was the beautiful Princess Leia. He blasted the door off with his pistol. "I'm Luke Skywalker," he announced. "I've come to rescue you. Ben Kenobi is with me."

"Ben Kenobi! Obi-wan! Where is he?"

Meanwhile, Governor Tarkin watched Darth Vader pace back and forth. "*He's* here," Vader said. "I can feel a stirring in the Force."

"*He*?" asked Tarkin. "You mean Obi-wan Kenobi? That's impossible. He must be dead by now."

A beeping intercom stopped Tarkin. It called out an alert in prisoner block AA-23. "The Princess!" Vader said. "I knew it. He *is* here. I must deal with him—alone."

Luke and Leia raced out of the prisoner's block, down a hallway, and right into a series of blinding explosions. Solo and Chewie came dashing towards them. "We can't go back that way," Han yelled.

The Princess was obviously irritated. "You've cut off our only escape route."

Solo glared. "I beg your pardon, Your Highness. Would you prefer to be back in your cell?"

Luke pulled out a small transmitter and called See Threepio. "Threepio, check the plans of this place on that computer. How can we get out of here?"

"Sorry, sir," replied Threepio. "All the exits are blocked."

"This is some rescue," the Princess said, grabbing Luke's pistol. "Follow me!" She fired at a small grate and plunged into a garbage chute.

Solo pushed Chewbacca down the chute and followed with Luke. As they slid down they could smell the awful stench of a roomful of garbage. They landed in the muck of the dim chamber. But they were not alone! Some sort of horrible creature was rumbling about beneath them. And then—Luke vanished!

"That creature's got him . . . shoot!" Leia screamed to Solo.

"Shoot what?" he said. "I can't see it."

As quickly as he had vanished, Luke appeared again.

"Han, it's O.K. . . . the creature let go. I guess it didn't care for me."

But then a new danger struck. With a sudden rumbling the walls began moving . . . closer and closer to each other. Luke and the others would be crushed in the garbage compactor!

Luke shouted into his transmitter, "Threepio! Threepio!"

Threepio was unable to answer. When troopers had blown up the computer he and Artoo were using, the robots had escaped and were now looking for another control panel.

The Princess, Chewie, Han, and Luke were only inches away from being crushed. Even Chewie's incredible strength couldn't stop walls.

"We're all going to be a lot thinner," Solo joked unhappily.

In the nick of time, Luke heard a voice on his intercom. "Sir? Sir? We've found another control panel." It was Threepio!

"Quick, Threepio, shut down the garbage compactor!" Luke shrieked.

Suddenly the walls stopped. Threepio could hear, through the happy cheers of his friends, Luke's words, "You did it! You did it! Threepio, we're all right. Now open the escape hatch."

Threepio pushed the right switch and the Princess, Chewie, Han, and Luke ran through an empty corridor overlooking the hangar. They could see the *Falcon.*

Luke called Threepio on his transmitter. "Threepio, are you and Artoo safe?"

"Yes, sir, but I'm worried about my old age. We had to abandon the computer room. We're in the main hangar, across from the *Falcon.*"

Luke couldn't see the robots. But they could see a dozen or more troopers going in and out of the freighter.

"Wow!" Han said. "Even if Kenobi knocked out the tractor beam, we're going to have a lot of trouble getting out of here."

Princess Leia saw the freighter for the first time. "You came here in that? You're braver than I thought."

Starting up the hallway, the Princess and her rescuers bumped into twenty Imperial troopers. Han immediately started to shoot, yelling and howling at the top of his lungs.

The unexpected attack surprised the troopers and they ran—with Han and Chewie at their heels. Luke and the Princess took off in another direction. Solo and Chewbacca chased the troopers till they reached a dead end. The troopers were forced to turn and face their pursuers. The startled Imperials realized they had been tricked. There were only two attackers!

"Oops . . . let's go, Chewie," Han shouted. "They're wise to us!"

The Imperials fired their blasters but Solo and Chewie outran them. They slipped through a corridor just before a shield door slammed shut.

"We made it, Chewie. We're safe . . . for now," Solo gasped.

During the fighting Ben Kenobi made his way to the highest point in the space station. He walked along a narrow, dangerous catwalk. One wrong step, and he would fall to his death. One sound, and he would be heard by the patrolling troopers. Ben almost merged with the darkness as he made his way to the tractor beam controls. He was unbelievably quiet as he tinkered with the wires and cables, disconnecting the tractor beam. He did it! The *Millennium Falcon* could escape!

Kenobi started to make his way back to the docking bay, dodging patrol after patrol. From all the commotion he heard, Ben knew his young friends had caused trouble on the station.

He was almost back to the *Falcon* when he sensed something familiar. He took one more cautious step. The black-caped figure loomed ominously before him. Darth Vader stepped from the shadows. "It's been a long time, Obi-wan Kenobi," he said solemnly.

A moment of silence passed. The two enemies ignited their lightsabers.

Luke and Leia raced down a hallway, dodging blasts from the troopers' guns.

"Quick!" Luke exclaimed. "Let's get to that hatchway. Maybe we can lock it and shake them."

Reaching the other side of the hatchway, Luke and the Princess stopped short on the edge of a bottomless pit. Across the opening was another hatchway that would probably lead them to the ship. But the bridge was gone.

Leia snapped the door shut so the troopers couldn't fire at them. "We've got to get across there somehow," she said.

Luke noticed a cable. With some luck they might be able to swing across. He whirled the cable! It fell short. He tried again. This time, success! The cable wrapped itself around some pipes and held tight. Luke wrapped the other end around his waist, grabbed the Princess, jumped, and swung across. *The Force was with them.* They landed safely on the other side and headed down a tunnel. Han Solo and Chewbacca had avoided the Imperials. They were waiting at the end of the tunnel. They could see the *Millennium Falcon* from where they stood.

Han smiled at Luke. "What kept you so long?"

"We met a few old friends," the Princess quipped.

Solo became serious. "To get aboard the freighter we'll still have to get past those guards."

"Look!" Leia cried.

In another tunnel leading to the docking area, Kenobi and Vader were fighting with their lightsabers. The flare of the sabers attracted the attention of the troopers, who ran to help Darth Vader. The *Millennium Falcon* was left ungarded.

"Now's our chance," Solo said. "Run!"

"They're headed for the ship, Artoo," said Threepio. "Come on, we're leaving!"

Obi-wan saw the troopers coming. He knew he was trapped.

The Dark Lord sneered. "You still have your skill, but your power has weakened. Prepare to meet the Force."

"This is a fight you cannot win, Darth. If my blade finds its mark, you will cease to exist. But if you cut me down, I will become more powerful. Heed my words." With a final and deliberate glance toward Luke, Obi-wan deactivated his lightsaber and stood quietly.

Vader was furious. He rushed forward, and with one spectacular slash, his saber seemed to cut Obi-wan in two. Kenobi's cloak fluttered to the ground. But Kenobi wasn't in it. He had vanished!

Solo and the others were almost at the ship when Ben fell. Luke screamed, "Ben!" and he and Solo began firing at the guards.

"It's too late, Luke," Leia shouted. "It's over."

"No!" Luke sobbed.

Just then, he heard Ben's voice. "Luke, listen. . . ." Luke turned and reluctantly followed the others into the *Millennium Falcon.*

The spaceship was moving. Solo and Chewbacca adjusted the controls. "I hope the old man knocked out that tractor beam," Solo said.

The ship flew through the door of the docking bay and out into free space. Nothing stopped it.

"He did it!" Solo called out.

Luke sat in the ship, dazed. The Princess tried to comfort him. "I can't believe he's gone," Luke whispered.

Chewbacca kept a close watch on the tracking screen. He growled something to Han Solo.

"Quick—come with me, kid," Solo yelled to Luke. "Chewie spotted fighter planes."

Luke didn't move. Solo came close. "Listen, Luke, Kenobi gave us this chance to get away. Do you want to waste it?"

Without a word, Luke followed Solo into a large, rotating bubble at the side of the ship. Huge weapons extended from the bubble. Han and Luke took their positions at the weapons and prepared for action.

"Here they come," Leia yelled.

Two fighters were approaching fast. Luke and Han kept a steady stream of fire. So did the fighters, but the *Falcon's* deflectors cushioned the blasts. One enemy bolt struck the freighter directly. It blew out a large control panel in the main passageway. Sparks flew in all directions.

Solo fixed a fighter in his gunsight. He fired. The fighter exploded. Luke's turn came next. Zzzap . . . another hit! He and Solo grinned at each other.

"There are two more fighters after us," reported Leia. "And we've already lost some monitors and a deflector shield."

"Don't worry," Luke told her. "The *Falcon* will hold together."

Luke blasted one of the fighters. The other one sped away.

"We've made it!" Leia shouted, and she hugged Chewbacca.

Darth Vader walked into the control room on Death Star. "Are they away?" he asked Governor Tarkin, who was studying a huge screen.

"They've just completed the jump to hyperspace. I hope your plan to let them go works, Vader."

"Don't worry. They will lead us to the Rebel base. This day will see the end of the Rebel Alliance," Darth Vader replied.

The *Millennium Falcon* was headed for one of the moons of a far-off planet called Yavin. Once, many thousands of years ago, men had lived on this moon and built a huge temple there. Now the temple was the Rebel headquarters.

As the *Falcon* set down near headquarters, a crowd of people rushed toward it. They were overjoyed to see the Princess. Their leader, Commander Willard, embraced Leia. "When we heard about Alderaan, we were afraid you had perished. I am so happy you are alive."

The Princess spoke quickly. "We must hurry, Commander. The Imperials on Death Star have surely tracked us here. You must use the information in Artoo to find a weakness in the battle station. It's our only hope."

Artoo Detoo had never felt so important. He was hooked up to dozens of computer outlets. The information tapes in Artoo were studied and evaluated. Finally, the Rebel leaders were ready. The Commander assembled the pilots and navigators in a large briefing room. Luke joined the pilots.

General Jan Dodonna spoke, "The Imperial battle station, Death Star, is approaching us from the far side of Yavin. We must stop it before it destroys us as it destroyed Alderaan. We think we have found its weakness.

"Death Star is completely secure against large spaceships," explained the General.

"However, the Imperials have never considered the danger from small fighters, like our X- and Y-wings. The station has a small thermal exhaust port. A direct hit on that port would start a chain reaction that would destroy Death Star."

"That's impossible," someone called out.

"It won't be easy," Dodonna admitted. "The fighter path is down a narrow trench. The target is small. We must make a direct hit. Blue squadron will cover for Red on the first run. Green will cover Gold on the second. Any questions?"

The room was silent.

"Then man your ships, and may the Force be with you."

The temple was bustling with activity. Luke walked toward his X-wing. He stopped when he reached Solo and Chewbacca. "You got your reward, Han, and now you're leaving?" Luke asked.

"That's right, kid. I have some debts to pay."

Luke was angry. "They could use a brave pilot like you, Han."

"Attacking that battle station isn't my idea of courage, Luke. It's more like suicide."

Luke turned away. "Well, take care of yourself, Han. But I guess that's what you do best."

Solo called after him. "Hey, Luke . . . may the Force be with you."

"What is it, Luke? What's wrong?" It was the Princess, waiting for him at his ship.

"It's Han. I thought he'd come."

"A man must follow his own path, Luke." Quickly Leia reached up and kissed him. "May the Force be with you," she said, and then she left.

Luke wished Ben were there. Just then, someone grabbed his arm. It was his old friend Biggs!

"Luke!" Biggs exclaimed. "We're flying together at last."

The two friends were joined by an older man known as Gold Leader. "Aren't you Luke Skywalker?" he asked. "I met your father once when I was just a boy. He was a great pilot."

There was no more time to talk. The pilots had to board their planes. Artoo Detoo was lifted into Luke's fighter. See Threepio looked sad.

"You'd better come back," he said to his little friend. "If you don't, who will I have to yell at?"

Luke touched a small lever. The X-wing began to move.

Princess Leia silently watched a display screen on which she could see Yavin and its moons.

General Dodonna spoke: "The large red dot shows where the battle station is. We have thirty minutes until it reaches us."

Now the X- and Y-wing fighters were in battle formation.

"This is it," called Gold Leader. "Let's go!"

They flew closer and closer to Death Star. Luke gasped as he approached that frightening black sphere again.

Gold Leader's voice came over the inter-ship pickup. "We're passing through their outer shields. Hold tight. Switch your deflectors on."

Gold Two, a pilot named Wedge Antilles, cried out, "Look at the size of that thing!"

Gold Leader was on the pickup again. "Red Leader, this is Gold Leader. It doesn't look like they're expecting us. You can go in. We'll keep them busy here."

"We're starting for the target now," Red Leader responded.

"May the Force be with you," Gold Leader called.

Alarm sirens sounded throughout Death Star. The Imperials couldn't believe their battle station was under attack. They fired every weapon they had against the Rebel ships—energy beams, electrical bolts, explosive solids.

"This is Gold Five," Luke announced. "I'm going in."

"I'm right behind you," Biggs answered.

Bolts flew from Luke's ship. With a flash, a huge fire began to burn. Luke shouted with terror as he realized he couldn't avoid the flames.

The heat was fierce, but the X-wing sped through the fire. "Wow!" Luke called to Biggs. "I've come through O.K.—just slightly toasted."

The Rebel X-wing ships hit a power terminal on the station. A Commander rushed up to Darth Vader. "We count at least thirty of them. They're so small and quick, we can't hit them."

"Get the TIE fighters ready," Vader said. "Mine too. We'll have to go after them ship by ship."

Biggs and Luke went in again. Luke's timing was better now. They were just pulling out when a call from the rebel command station came. "Squad leaders, attention. Enemy fighters are heading your way."

A minute later, Luke shouted, "Biggs . . . you've picked one up. On your tail. Watch it!"

"He's on me tight. I can't shake him," Biggs called.

Luke zoomed around and got behind the TIE.

"Hang on. I'm coming."

Zzzap! Luke fired. The TIE exploded. Biggs was safe. Gold Six was not so lucky. A TIE hit him.

In the Rebel headquarters at the temple, something went wrong with the big screen.

"Switch to audio," Leia snapped. She was worried about the fighters, particularly Gold Five, Luke. She thought he was taking too many chances.

The control room was filled with the calls from plane to plane and the roars of blasts and explosions.

"Watch your back, Luke," Biggs shouted.

"I can't shake him. He's too close," Luke yelled.

"Hold on. I'm on him," Wedge cried.

The TIE vanished.

"Thanks, Wedge," Luke whispered.

"Gold Leader, this is Red Leader. We're starting our attack. No enemy fighters up here yet. Looks like we'll get one good run."

As the Rebel Y-fighters started for the trench, the Imperial crew stationed there began to shoot faster and faster. Bolts exploded everywhere. Then the firing stopped.

"Why?" wondered Red Two.

Red Five made a guess. "Watch for enemy fighter planes."

His guess was right. Within seconds the TIE fighters attacked. Red Two, Red Five, and Red Leader were shot down by Vader and his men.

"Gold Boys, this is Gold Leader. Report in."

The calls came.

"Gold Two."

"Gold Ten."

"Gold Five. I have a TIE on my tail."

Luke maneuvered sharply, but couldn't shake the fighter. He was glad to hear Biggs say, "I see you, Luke." He looked around, but didn't see Biggs anywhere.

To Luke's surprise—and to the TIE fighter's—Biggs soared in from the front and blasted the fighter. "My turn to help you, pal," Biggs shouted happily.

Then General Dodonna made an announcement. "Gold Leader, you're going in. Keep half of your group ready to make the next run."

"Copy, Gold Leader. May the Force be with you. Biggs, Wedge, let's close up."

The two pilots joined Luke to wait their turn.

Gold Leader sped through the trench. Gold Ten and Gold Twelve were close behind.

"Keep your eyes open for fighters," Gold Leader warned.

"They're coming in. Point three five," Luke called.

Gold Twelve exploded under Vader's deadly fire.

"Hurry, Gold Leader. I can't hold them long," Gold Ten shouted.

"Almost there," Gold Leader whispered. "Fire!"

It was close but not close enough. The torpedoes hit only the surface of the target. Neither plane got out of the trench. Imperial fighters hit them. Gold Leader's last words were, "Start your run, Gold Five."

Luke, Biggs, and Wedge went in at full speed. Luke heard a familiar voice in his ears. "Trust your feelings, Luke," it said. Luke couldn't believe what he had heard. It was Ben Kenobi's voice.

Energy bolts were exploding wildly. The Imperial fighters were in hot pursuit.

"Almost at target," Luke called.

He let his torpedoes fly. With two powerful roars, they hit—but way off target.

"Pull up," he screamed.

The TIE fighters were hot on their tails. Luke saw them.

"Wedge, Biggs, split up."

The three raced in different directions. The TIE fighters followed Luke. One of the pilots was Darth Vader. He fired, but missed.

"The Force is strong in that one," he said to himself.

He nicked Luke's plane with an energy bolt, but Artoo fixed the damage in seconds.

"O.K., we're going in," Luke informed the other two.

Now he heard the voice again. "Let's go, Luke."

Biggs and Wedge crisscrossed in back of Luke, trying to confuse the Imperials.

"Hurry, Luke," Biggs called. "They're coming in faster this time."

Vader fired again. This time he struck Biggs. The plane burst into a million glowing splinters. Luke choked back tears. He said softly, "We're a couple of shooting stars, Biggs. We'll never be stopped."

Just then, Wedge signaled. "Something's wrong with my plane, Luke. I can't stay with you."

Now there was only Luke . . . with three TIE fighters on his tail. He was doomed. Then—an explosion! Something hit one of the TIEs and it went up in flames. A familiar Corellian spaceship appeared from nowhere and blasted the TIE. It crossed daringly in front of the two remaining planes, upsetting them so violently that they crashed. One exploded. The other—Vader's—went hurtling off into space.

The shout was from Han Solo: "You're all clear now, kid. Blow up this battle station so we can all go home."

Another voice sounded in Luke's head. "Trust me, Luke."

Luke let his feelings take over. He scarcely remembered firing the torpedoes, but the cheering voices told him he had.

"You did it! You did it!" screamed Wedge.

"Good shot, kid," Solo yelled.
Chewie howled with delight.
Then Luke saw the light as bright as a sun. Death Star was gone. Luke turned his plane toward Yavin.

A cheering crowd welcomed the pilots. The Rebel Alliance had won. They would bring justice back to the Empire.

"I knew you'd come back, Han. I knew it!" Luke shouted.

"Well, I couldn't leave you to take all the credit . . . and all the reward," Han said.

Chewie clapped Luke on the back with such enthusiasm that Luke almost fell over. Only Threepio was sad. His little friend Artoo was in terrible shape from one of the hits Luke's plane had taken.

"Oh, my!" he exclaimed. "Artoo, can you hear me? Please be all right."

Threepio was assured that Artoo just needed a few new circuits. He would be back in the blink in no time.

The Princess was bursting with pride. She hugged Luke and Han, shouting, "You did it! You did it!"

The next day, a great ceremony was held in a beautiful chamber in the temple. Everyone assembled . . . the Senators, generals, troops . . . everyone who had fought so hard and so well for the Rebel cause.

Han and Luke walked solemnly down the aisle, followed by Chewbacca. Princess Leia stood on a high platform. Looking more beautiful than ever, she placed chains of honor on Han and Luke. They were heroes. The crowd cheered. The war was over . . . the Force would be with them all.